WILDFIRE!

By Annie Auerbach
Illustrated by S. I. International Illustrators

LITTLE SIMON
New York   London   Toronto   Sydney

LITTLE SIMON

An imprint of Simon & Schuster Children's Publishing Division

1230 Avenue of the Americas

New York, New York 10020

Copyright © 2004 Mattel, Inc. MATCHBOX and all associated logos are trademarks

owned by and used under license from Mattel, Inc. All rights reserved.

LITTLE SIMON and colophon are registered trademarks of Simon & Schuster.

All rights reserved, including the right of reproduction in whole or in part in any form.

Manufactured in the United States of America

First Edition

2   4   6   8   10   9   7   5   3   1

ISBN 0-689-86728-X

CRACK! ZAP!

In a remote area of the Whitman Forest lightning had struck a towering tree. It split the tree right down the middle, sending it falling to the ground. But the worst was yet to come. The tree had landed on some dry brush, and the immense heat from the lightning had sparked a fire. Not just any fire. . . . A wildfire!

Meanwhile fire chief Michael Woller was driving into work to begin his shift. Fire season was here which meant the weather was warm, the land was dry, and the firefighters were extremely busy. Fighting wildland fires was much harder than fighting house fires, because they were much harder to contain. But according to Michael and the brave men and women that did it, that was exactly what made the job exciting.

"Good morning," Michael said to the dispatcher. "What's the latest?"

"Ah, Chief Woller. Good timing," said the dispatcher. "One of our pilots just reported that he spotted a fire in the Whitman Forest about ten miles south of Vandelay Ridge."

"Boy, it's never dull around here," Michael said to the dispatcher with a wink. Then he made his way outside where there was already a flurry of activity. He found Alicia, one of the pilots.

"Let's try and contain this fire as fast as we can," Michael said. "While I assemble a team here I'd like you and Sam to use the water bomber."

This huge plane was able to drop liquid fire retardant, or fire-stopping chemicals, in front of the fire to slow its progress.

Alicia and her copilot, Sam, scrambled to the cockpit and prepared for takeoff.

Once they were soaring in the air, Alicia and Sam flew east. Using a device on the plane that detects warmth, they could zero in on where the fire was and could see how many acres had already been consumed. It was up to them to try and prevent the fire from spreading farther.

"Ready?" Alicia asked Sam through the headset.

Sam nodded. "Let's blanket those flames!"

The water bomber cruised at a lower altitude. In less than fifteen
seconds fire retardant was dropped from the plane in a great sweeping line.

But their job wasn't over yet—for this fire had no intention of stopping anytime soon.

"Is it water time?" Sam asked.

Alicia gave a thumbs-up.

The water bomber was true to its name and could hold up to 1,400 gallons of water—another perfect enemy of fire.

The water bomber was flown to a nearby lake. Since it had wheels *and* floats, the water bomber could land on the ground or on the water. "Lower the water pickup probes," Alicia instructed Sam.

WHOOSH!

At a powerful speed the water bomber skimmed the surface of the lake. In only twelve seconds the plane had scooped up enough water to refill its tanks!

"Retract the pickup probes, and let's get back to the fire to do another drop," said Alicia.

"You got it," replied Sam.

At the same time as the water bomber was doing its job, everyone else back at the fire station was gearing up.

"Suit up, people!" Michael yelled. "Let's get on the plane! That fire's going to spread rapidly."

Swiftly the crew of sixteen boarded the cargo plane and headed toward the raging fire. The forest was no place for a fire truck. These were no ordinary firefighters. These were smoke jumpers! Smoke jumpers relied on a plane to take them to the heart of the fire.

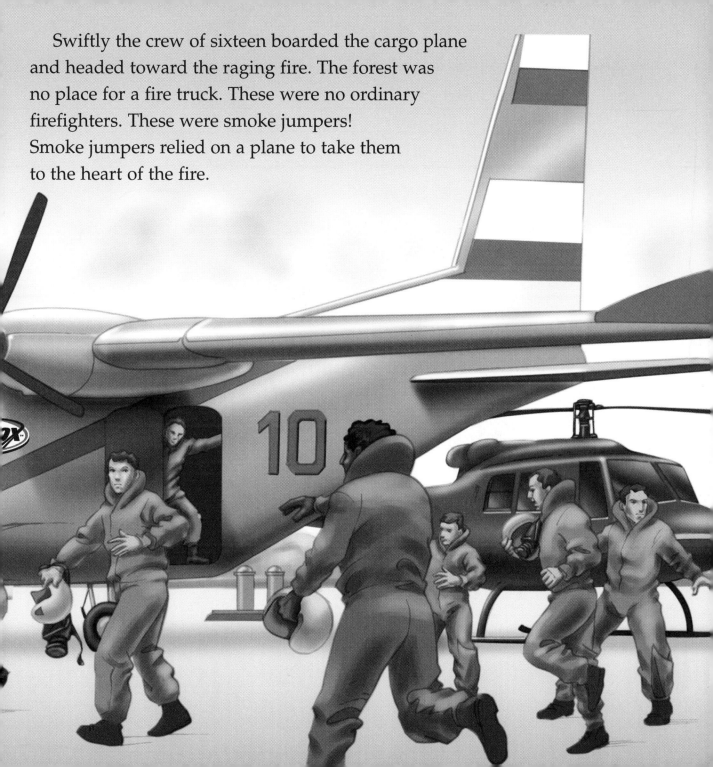

Once the plane took off, Marc was the spotter. It was his job to determine the best place to jump. He looked for the colored retardant released by the water bomber. When that was detected, Marc threw down weighted paper streamers to test the wind's speed and direction.

When the plane climbed to 3,000 feet it was jump time!

Two by two, the smoke jumpers parachuted out of the plane. The pilot made several trips over the same site, with parachuting firefighters jumping out each time. The smoke jumpers landed amongst the trees and then lowered themselves down with rope.

The plane then dropped speed and altitude. Marc pushed out boxes of supplies that were attached to parachutes. Once that was complete the pilot headed off to see how rapidly the fire was spreading. Michael and the other firefighters disengaged from their parachutes and quickly retrieved the supplies of water, food, and tools.

"Let's start over here," called Michael. He began clearing a path to make a fire line. "If there's no brush for the fire to feed on, it will hopefully stop burning."

The firefighters got to work, digging and shoveling, and trying to avoid the smoke that seemed to be thickening in the air.

CRACKLE! SIZZLE! POP! SNAP!

The fire was growing larger and fiercer by the minute. The fire line that had been created was holding back part of the fire, but up in the cargo plane Marc watched as the fire roared through the forest, consuming everything in its path.

He radioed to Michael. "Before you know it, the flames are going to be dangerously close to you."

"Thanks for the heads-up," Michael said. He radioed into dispatch. "We need backup. I think it's time to call up the volunteers. And we need the water bomber again," he said. "This fire is tough."

The water bomber was needed so Alicia and Sam were back in the air. The plane's tanks had been refilled, and they dropped another massive line of retardant over the intense flames. They repeated this procedure many times, alternating between water and fire retardant.

Daytime turned into nighttime, and soon three days had passed! Gallons and gallons of water and fire retardant had been dropped. Nearly one hundred firefighters were risking their lives to save the forest and wildlife that lived there.

Finally the fire was contained and mostly extinguished. It had been an intense few days, but it had also been a time of firefighting heroes—be it the firefighters themselves or the aircraft that helped them save the forest.

"Great work," Michael told everyone. "Amazing teamwork all around." Then he laughed and added, "This certainly isn't a boring job, is it?"

"That's for sure!" the others agreed.